LOUISE,
Soccer
Star?

LOUISE, Soccer Star?

by STEPHEN KRENSKY
pictures by SUSANNA NATTI

PUFFIN BOOKS

PUFFIN BOOKS
Published by the Penguin Group
Penguin Putnam Books for Young Readers,
345 Hudson Street, New York, New York 10014, U.S.A.
Penguin Books Ltd, 80 Strand, London WC2R ORL, England
Penguin Books Australia Ltd, Ringwood, Victoria, Australia
Penguin Books Canada Ltd, 10 Alcorn Avenue, Toronto, Ontario, Canada M4V 3B2
Penguin Books (N.Z.) Ltd, 182-190 Wairau Road, Auckland 10, New Zealand

Penguin Books Ltd, Registered Offices: Harmondsworth, Middlesex, England

First published in the United States of America by Dial Books for Young Readers,
a division of Penguin Putnam Inc., 2000
Published by Puffin Books,
a division of Penguin Putnam Books for Young Readers, 2002

1 3 5 7 9 10 8 6 4 2

THE LIBRARY OF CONGRESS HAS CATALOGED THE DIAL EDITION AS FOLLOWS:
Krensky, Stephen.
Louise, soccer star? / by Stephen Krensky; pictures by Susanna Natti.
p. cm.
Summary: Louise's love of soccer and her high hopes for the new season
are tested when she feels overshadowed by a talented new player.
ISBN: 0-8037-2495-0 (hc)
[1. Soccer—Fiction.] I. Natti, Susanna, ill. II. Title.
PZ7.K883 Lmk 2000
[Fic]—dc21 99-048535

Puffin Books ISBN 0-14-230139-6

Printed in the United States of America

CHAPTER 1

"Go! Go! Go!"

The words rang through Louise Page's head as she sprinted down the soccer field, dribbling the ball expertly through a clutch of midfielders—left, right, left, right. . . . The ball never strayed more than a few inches from her foot.

Suddenly, the fullbacks charged. Louise dodged one, then another. Ahead, the defending sweeper was moving forward, trying to contain her.

Just a little closer, thought Louise. That's *it*. . . .

As the sweeper closed in, Louise threw a quick head fake and blew by her.

The crowd in the stands rose to its feet.

"LOU-ISE! LOU-ISE!"

Though she couldn't help hearing her name, Louise remained focused. She looked around quickly to pass. Assist or goal, it made no difference to her. Unfortunately, her blazing speed had left her teammates far behind.

"Oh, well," she murmured, "they're trying their best. But it's time for action—and I *won't* let them down."

Just then, the stopper tried to force her to the outside. Louise did a quick stutter step and a spinning reverse cut. The stopper tried to keep up but, dazzled by Louise's deft moves, she tripped over her own feet.

"LOU-ISE!"

She was now in the goal area. Just ahead, she could see the goalie sweating, nervously shifting her weight from one foot to the other.

Cool and collected, Louise smiled. At this

distance, her aim was deadly.

The crowd was shouting again.

"LOU-ISE! LOU-ISE!"

Eyes glued to the goal, Louise focused on the far post. She pulled back her foot, prepared to strike.

"LOU-ISE! How many times do I have to call you?"

Louise sighed. She opened her eyes and looked up from her bed. The crowd, the soccer field, and her soon-to-be goal all faded away.

"What is it, Mother?"

Mrs. Page was standing in the doorway. "Are you ready?"

"I just have to put on my cleats."

"Your soccer practice starts in ten minutes. We don't want to be late."

Louise reached forward and pulled on her shin guards. She smiled up at the wall, where a poster of the Women's U.S.A. World Cup champions beamed back at her.

Her younger brother, Lionel, appeared at the door.

"Still not ready? You know, Louise, you're taking a big chance."

"I am? How come?"

"By not getting to your practice early. All the lucky uniform numbers will be taken before you get there."

Louise held up her hand. "I'm not worried. Everybody knows I like number 7. That's always been my number. Nobody else will take it."

"You can't be so sure what some people will do," Lionel insisted. "So just remember, I warned you."

Louise waved off his concern. She had been preparing for this day all summer. What could possibly go wrong?

CHAPTER 2

It was only a short ride to the soccer field, but Louise spent the whole time drumming her fingers on the armrest.

"Can't we go any faster?" she asked.

"*Now* you're in a hurry," said her mother.

"I guess I am."

Mrs. Page smiled. "You've really been looking forward to this season, haven't you?"

Louise nodded. Last year she had been among the younger players on her team. It had been hard to keep up with the bigger, faster girls.

But this year would be different. This year

Louise and her friends would be the bigger, faster kids.

As they reached the town soccer fields, they saw three team practices going on.

"Which one is yours?" asked Mrs. Page.

"Over there. To the right. I see Emily and Megan. Um, can you let me out here?"

"Afraid I'll embarrass you?" Her mother sighed. "And here I went to the trouble of removing the spinach from between my teeth."

Louise rolled her eyes. "See you later, Mother."

She ran over to join her friends. Megan was busy computing the odds of scoring from midfield. She was very good with numbers and could make an equation out of almost any situation.

"I suppose wind velocity would play a part," she said. "Not to mention the barometric pressure."

"If you say so," said Emily. "Hey, Louise, we were beginning to wonder. The uniforms are over there." She pointed to a box on the grass.

Louise rummaged through it. "Number 7 is gone!"

"Don't look at me," said Emily. "I've got 9."

"Mine's 13," said Megan.

Louise looked around. "There it is—on some new girl."

"That's Trelawney Hunt," said Emily. "She just moved into town."

"Tre-hooey?"

"Tre-lawn-ey," Emily repeated. "It's a British name. Which makes sense because Trelawney is from England."

"Well, then, I guess she couldn't know about me and my number 7. I'd better go talk to her about it."

This new girl was bouncing a soccer ball from one knee to the other and then down to her foot.

Louise watched in awe. Trelawney made it look so easy. Louise always felt like a jerky wind-up toy when she tried it herself.

"Excuse me," she said. "I think you took my shirt by accident."

Trelawney trapped the ball. "I did?"

"You see, number 7 is special to me. Good luck, you might say."

Trelawney bounced the ball on her right foot. Once, twice, three times. "I didn't realize you could reserve a certain number."

"You can't, exactly," Louise admitted. She hesitated. How could she put what she was feeling into words?

"Never mind," Trelawney went on. "I'll let you have it. My name's Trelawney, by the way. Trelawney Hunt. My mum just got transferred over here to the States."

"Hi. I'm Louise Page. Um, welcome to America. And never mind about the shirt."

"Really, you can have it."

Now that Trelawney was offering the shirt, Louise felt funny about taking it. The shirt would probably like being with Trelawney because she was such a good player. "No thanks. I couldn't take it now," she said.

"Why not? I've only just put it on. It isn't even sweaty yet."

"I know, but it's, um, bonded with you already. It would be bad luck to change things now."

"I've never heard of that. Is it an American custom?"

Actually, it was only Louise's custom, but she didn't want to explain that. It was hard enough to accept that the soccer season had barely begun—and she was already starting off on the wrong foot.

CHAPTER 3

"Rats! Rats! And more rats!"

Emily laughed. "Sounds like a plague to me. Come on, now, Louise, it wasn't *that* bad."

They were standing with Megan after school. That morning Mr. Hathaway had asked Louise to give Trelawney a tour of the school. Then he sat the two of them at adjoining desks.

"Your face is all red, Louise," Emily added.

Megan agreed. "I estimate your blood pressure is up 20%. You should try to calm down."

Louise continued to pace. "Calm down? Hah! Did you see the coach actually rubbing

her hands together? She was so pleased. *'Trelawney can show us'* this and *'Trelawney can show us'* that."

"But that wasn't Trelawney's fault, and she actually looked pretty uncomfortable about the whole thing."

"I guess. But remember last year, when *we* were smaller than all the older kids in the league? Well, this is supposed to be *our* big chance."

"I remember you wanted to play center forward," said Emily.

Louise nodded. "That's right! And I would if it weren't for her. First she takes my number, then my soccer position."

"Or *football* position, as she probably calls it," Megan added. "Actually, it's called football or *futbol* in almost every country in the world. It's just here in the United States that we insist on—"

"Megan, that's not the point," Louise went on. "I just want to know why this had to happen to *me*."

"It didn't exactly happen to you," Megan reminded her. "I mean, Trelawney didn't single you out."

Louise sighed. "That's easy for you to say. Trelawney isn't a goalie, like you are."

"Well, if it makes you feel any better, Trelawney won't be here forever."

"She won't?"

"Uh-uh. She told me that her mother's company only transferred her here for five years."

Louise gasped. "Five years! I'm supposed to feel better because Trelawney Hunt will *only* be here until we're in high school?"

Emily shook her head. "Oh, Louise, things aren't that bad. Besides, it's exciting to have such a good player on the team. We might even win a few games."

Louise snorted. "Well, Coach always says winning isn't everything."

"True," Emily admitted, "but it could make for a nice change."

Louise just bit her lip. "And do you know what's even worse?" she said, sighing.

"No, what?"

"She's *nice*. I mean, the whole time I was taking her around, she was *so* friendly. Why couldn't she be all mean or snobby?"

Megan looked quickly in both directions. "It must be part of a master plan to ruin your life."

"Yes," Louise said firmly, "that *must* be it."

CHAPTER 4

The first game of the season always made Louise feel funny. Somehow these official games seemed so different from the ones played at recess. There was this feeling of being in the spotlight, of having everyone watching you. Of course, that made the game more exciting too.

Louise's parents and Lionel were all at the game. On the one hand, Louise liked to have her family cheering for her. On the other hand, there was always the very real danger of being embarrassed—like once when her father had shouted, "Totally awesome, Louise!" after she had just made a simple pass up the line. Of course, what made it even worse was hearing words like *totally* and *awesome* coming out of her parents' mouths.

"Come on, Lou-ise!" her mother yelled as the referee blew the whistle to start the game.

For the first few minutes, neither team had a shot on goal. The ball just ping-ponged back and forth on the field.

Then a long goal kick bounced toward Louise at midfield. As she trapped it, Trelawney broke toward the middle. Louise considered a quick cross, but hesitated.

Thunnnk!

A defender kicked the ball out from between her legs.

Her teammates groaned.

"Shake it off, Louise!"

"Keep your head in the game."

Twweeeet!

The whistle sounded the end of the first half with the score still 0–0. The coach huddled the team together.

"I know it's early in the season," she said, "but we need to look out for each other a bit more. Remember what Benjamin Franklin said: 'If we don't hang together, then surely we will all hang separately.'"

Louise turned to Trelawney. "He said that right before the American Revolution."

Trelawney laughed. "Just a little before my time."

In the second half Trelawney unloaded one strong shot. Then another. And a third. But each time, the opposing goalie managed to block the shot.

"Try to contain them!" the coach yelled. "Don't let them get by you."

Things would be different if I were center forward, Louise thought. She was so ready to charge down the field, to dart fearlessly in and out and head the ball into the goal. But that was the center forward's job—Trelawney's job. So instead Louise shuffled up and down the field until she was taken out for a rest.

The game ended in a 1–1 tie. Both teams seemed relieved to have escaped without a loss.

"That new player is really something," said Mr. Page as they drove off. "What's that tricky thing she does?"

"It's called a *rainbow*," Lionel explained. "You have to kick the ball with your heels so that it comes back over your head. No one else in the whole school can do it. And did you see the way she headed in the tying goal? She's amazing."

"Do we have to talk about this now?" Louise asked.

Her mother frowned. "You're a little grumpy, aren't you? After all, a tie isn't so bad."

Mr. Page rubbed his forehead. "Heading the ball always looks like it hurts. Anyway, Lionel, no one player wins the game alone. Or ties it either. It's a team effort. Right, Louise?"

Louise had scrunched herself up in the

backseat. "I guess," she said. Louise knew teamwork was important, but she wanted to stand out at the same time.

So far, she hadn't even come close.

CHAPTER 5

The next morning at school Louise found herself approaching the back of a large crowd.

"What's going on?" she asked. "Was there an accident? Is somebody hurt?"

Emily turned around. "Jasper made a bet with Trelawney that she couldn't bounce a soccer ball off her knees twenty times before it hit the ground."

"How's she doing?" asked Louise. Even with hours of practice, her personal record was only eight.

"Let's go and see," said Emily. Both girls squirmed forward for a better look.

"Eighteen, nineteen, twenty," Trelawney said. She caught the ball in her hands.

"I can't believe it," said Jasper. "On the first try too. You're sure you're not a professional?"

Trelawney smiled. "Just an amateur in good standing."

More than good standing, thought Louise. Twenty was *very* impressive.

"Do you think you could show me how to do that?" Jasper asked.

"Sure. Start like this. . . ."

Emily put her hand on Louise's shoulder.

"Louise, are you feeling okay? You look a little pale."

Louise smiled weakly. "I'll be fine. Hey, do you want to come over after school today? I've got the new issue of *Soccer Monthly*. We could take another look at that World Cup video, you know, for pointers."

"Sorry," said Emily. "Trelawney invited me over." She paused. "But you could probably come too. I'll ask—"

"No, no," said Louise. "You go ahead."

In class, Mr. Hathaway began a lesson on the Greek myths. It turned out to be a subject Trelawney had already studied. When Mr. Hathaway asked for impressions of life on Mt. Olympus, she rattled off descriptions of the gods and goddesses without pausing for breath. She even worked in a joke about Zeus' lightning bolts of inspiration.

At lunch, Trelawney joined the girls at their usual table.

"Are castles as cold as they look?" Megan asked, taking a bite from her sandwich.

Trelawney shivered. "Worse," she said. "And damp too. Not to mention all those chamber pots." She held up her milk carton. "A toast to modern plumbing."

"Hear, hear," said Emily.

"There's something I've always wanted to know," Louise broke in. "Does steak-and-kidney pie have real kidney in it?"

"Of course," said Trelawney. "It's a key ingredient."

"I think there was some kidney in yesterday's mystery glop," said Megan.

Louise looked down at her sandwich, which she was relieved to see was good old peanut butter and jelly.

But even peanut butter and jelly didn't seem to help Louise much during the afternoon soccer practice. The coach played her in different positions, but in each one Louise just shuffled along.

If I were center forward, things would be different, thought Louise. I'd be a blur, a flash, a gust—

The coach blew her whistle.

"Louise, where are you going?"

Louise looked puzzled. "I was just dribbling down the wing."

"But, Louise, you're going the wrong way!"

Louise felt her face turning bright red.

Some of the other girls laughed, but most kept their eyes on the ground.

"Enough, enough," the coach warned them. "Louise, unturn yourself and get into the game."

Louise nodded. But she couldn't help feeling a little lost. Everything seemed to be going downhill lately. Enough, she decided, was definitely enough.

It was time to bounce back.

CHAPTER 6

The front door of the Pages' house slammed shut.

"Is that you, Louise?" Mrs. Page called out.

Louise grunted.

"Hmmm," her mother went on. "An after-school grunt. Definitely not a good sign. Can we talk about it?"

Louise grunted again. Twice.

"I'll take that as a no. But let me know if you change your mind."

Louise made herself a snack. Then she plopped down in front of the computer to play Trek, her favorite adventure game. Usually she could forget about the real world while maneuvering through Trek's tricky terrain. But today even successfully passing through the Forest of Terrifying Trees didn't help.

She closed down the game and turned on the TV instead.

"*Welcome to* The Muscle Hustle. *Our guest today is going to demonstrate new ways to build muscles and increase coordination.*"

"*That's right, Biff. Instead of joining an expensive health club or buying fancy equipment, why not integrate household activities into an effective strength-and-conditioning program?*"

Louise sat up. Now this sounded interesting. If she could build up her muscles and endurance, the team would have to make room for more than one star. She grabbed a pen and started taking notes.

A short while later Louise stood in her driveway checking off the items on her list—a hose, a bucket of soapy water, a backpack full of books.

She started sponging the car's hood in a circular motion. The backpack weighed her down, making it harder to move. But when she returned to the soccer field, her muscles would be primed for action.

"Wow!"

Lionel was standing at the edge of the driveway. "What did you do?" he went on.

Louise put down the hose. "What do you mean?"

"It must have been something really terrible to get such a punishment."

"Lionel, I'm not being punished."

Her brother laughed. "Oh, I suppose it was *your* idea to wash the car?"

"That's right."

Lionel took a step back. "Is this some kind of weird disease?"

"I'm not sick, Lionel. I'm building up my cardiovascular system."

"Is that dangerous?"

"No, Lionel. It just means I'm creatively increasing my endurance."

"But you're still washing the car, right?" Lionel squinted at her. "Are you *sure* you're the real Louise?"

"Yes, Lionel, I'm the real Louise, the one who's getting tired of all these silly questions."

"That still doesn't—"

"Enough, Lionel! Just stay out of my way. Unless, of course," she added darkly, picking up the hose, "you feel like being washed too."

CHAPTER 7

"You might think," Mr. Hathaway was saying, "that given their many powers the Greek gods and goddesses would have been happy and easygoing. But the gods were all too human in their loves and hates, in their strengths and weaknesses. None of them were very forgiving, and revenge was ultimately their favorite sport. Zeus, after all, had come to power by betraying and imprisoning his own father. So it wasn't surprising that they all spent so much time looking over their shoulders. Yes, Emily?"

"I know that some gods didn't get along at all. Which ones were they?"

Mr. Hathaway laughed. "It's a long list. As the god of war, Ares was always very touchy and loved to start fights. But jealousy between gods was the biggest problem. For example, Hera was Zeus' wife and the mother of many other gods and goddesses. But Athena simply sprang from Zeus' forehead one day. So Hera couldn't claim any credit for her. Her sudden arrival caught Hera by surprise."

Louise stole a look at Trelawney. She knew what that felt like.

* * *

At lunch Emily, Megan, Trelawney, and Louise were still discussing the different myths.

"I'd like to be one of those Titans," said Emily. "Can you see me as a giant walking the earth?"

"Yes," said Louise. "Stepping on the rest of us and squashing us like bugs."

Emily considered this. "What would be the odds of stepping on someone, Megan?"

Megan considered the problem. "Maybe 38%. Of course, we'd have some warning, considering the Titans' shadows and the vibrations they made as they walked. So maybe we could avoid getting squished."

"Things didn't work out that way in *Rex on the Rampage*," Louise reminded them.

Megan groaned.

Emily shook her head.

"I loved that movie!" said Trelawney.

Louise was surprised. "You did?"

"Oh, yes. I especially liked the first part, when the Tyrannosaurus destroys Tokyo."

"No, no," said Louise. "First the dinosaur trashes New York. Then Tokyo."

Trelawney shook her head. "I don't think so."

"Trelawney, I've seen this movie five times. I know which city gets flattened—"

"Wait a minute, Louise," said Emily. "I think Tokyo *is* destroyed first."

"That's right," said Megan. "Because after Tokyo the dinosaur has a giant metal splinter in his paw. And it gets knocked out against the Empire State Building."

Louise blinked. She had forgotten about that splinter. Trelawney was right and she was wrong—again.

"I guess," she said abruptly, and was very quiet after that.

Louise went home alone that afternoon. Emily had offered to play, but Louise had told her that she had errands to do.

After consulting her notes, Louise started on the next phase of her conditioning.

"Louise, what's going on?"

"What does it look like, Lionel?"

"It looks like you're cleaning the house."

"Wrong again, Lionel. This is a muscle-conditioning follow-up."

"I guess that explains why you filled your pockets with sand."

"How did you . . ." She looked around. "Oh, I guess I am leaking a little. . . ."

Lionel backed away. "First the car and now

this. Whatever you're infected with, I hope *I* don't catch it!"

Louise ignored him. "I am Hera," she told herself, huffing and puffing as she went up and down the stairs. "And when I get done, all of Olympus, especially Athena, will know my power!"

CHAPTER 8

The leaf caught Louise's eye as it fluttered to the ground.

Wait . . . wait . . .

At the last second Louise swung out with her foot, trying to kick the leaf with her big toe. It was the next step of her program—*practicing her conditioning in an unfamiliar environment.*

"Louise goes for the loose ball. . . ."

The leaf caught the edge of her sneaker.

"She fights off a defender to chip toward midfield. . . ."

Louise took another swing. *Missed!*

"Rats!" she muttered. That was twelve misses in a row!

The grass was covered with leaves that had fallen earlier. Starting in one corner, Louise began pushing them around. She did several sweeps with her right foot, then an equal number with her left.

"Hey, Louise!"

Megan came running up to her. "Your mother

said you were back here. What are you doing?"

Louise folded her arms. "It's kind of like yard work, but not exactly."

Megan looked at the scattered line of leaves. "Hmmmm. It almost looks like you're raking. Of course, it might help if you were actually holding a rake."

Louise knew she had to say something. "Oh, sure, I could use a rake," she said. "But this way it's more like soccer practice. I'm swinging my foot a lot."

Megan smiled. "Does that really help?"

"It's an experiment, really. If you want to practice too, there's plenty of leaves to go around."

Megan shook her head. "Thanks, but no thanks. I mean, don't get me wrong, Louise. I like soccer. I just don't love it like you do. Anyway, I came over to see if you wanted to go downtown."

Louise surveyed the leaf-covered lawn.

"Thanks. But I've still got lots more practic-ing to do."

"Okay. Well, I'll see you later. Hi, Mr. Page."

"Hello yourself, Megan," said Louise's father, coming around the corner. "Any good odds to report today?"

"Not yet. But it's early. There's an 83% chance of a prediction before nightfall. Bye."

Mr. Page waited till Megan was out of sight. Then he spoke up.

"Louise, I think we need to talk."

Louise looked up at her father's face. She knew what his *we-need-to-talk* voice meant. She wasn't in trouble exactly, but he was bothered by something she was doing, something that should be changed.

"Couldn't we talk later?" she asked. "I'm kind of in the middle of things."

"No excuses, Louise," said Mr. Page. "It's about your behavior lately. Now, don't get me wrong. The house has never looked better."

Louise kept sweeping, but her foot slowed a little.

"It's the reason behind all this that I'm concerned about."

"What did Lionel tell you?" she asked.

"Enough. And I'm glad he did. You know, Louise, I usually think you tackle your problems constructively. But here you seem to be a little, um, over-sensitive—"

"I am not!" Louise snapped. "I just thought

this season was going to be my chance to show what I could do. And then along comes Trelawney to mess things up."

Mr. Page frowned. "Hold on a minute, Louise. Just because Trelawney's a good player doesn't mean you can't be too. I'm sure the team can use as many good players as possible."

"I still think *my* friends should take *my* side."

Her father smiled. "Louise, I'll bet they don't even know they haven't. Adding a new friend doesn't have to mean getting rid of old ones. And put yourself in Trelawney's place—new town, new classmates, new country. That must be pretty hard."

Louise opened her mouth to speak, but no words came out. She knew her father was right, but knowing it and admitting it were not the same thing.

"It just doesn't seem fair," she said finally.

"I can understand that," her father said.

"Please don't agree with me," said Louise. "I can't argue with you if you agree with me."

Her father smiled. "I know. That's one of the best strategies in *The Father's Handbook*."

Louise folded her arms. "You're always mentioning that book. I'd like to see it sometime."

Mr. Page shook his head. "Not allowed. Definitely not allowed."

"Well, that's not fair either."

"Maybe. Or maybe it all depends on how you look at it. Most things are that way."

"Yes," Louise agreed reluctantly. They definitely were.

CHAPTER 9

Louise stood amid the swirl of clouds at midfield. All around her, the gods and goddesses were warming up for the game. Zeus and Hera were the opposing coaches. The three Fates were the referees, which made sense since they were the only ones who didn't fear Zeus and his thunderbolts.

Louise had been invited to participate because the gods had decided that she was just too good to play with mere mortals. Off to the left she saw Hermes, the messenger, lapping the field on his winged feet. Poseidon, god of the sea, was in goal. All that swimming had given him arms that seemed to be everywhere—she had heard his teammates call him "the octopus."

"Hey, Louise!"

Louise blinked—and the gods and goddesses faded away.

Emily was standing over her.

"Didn't you hear the coach? We're supposed to do a warm-up lap before the game starts."

As Louise sprinted around the field, she imagined herself having the speed of Hermes and the strength of Hercules. That would surely impress the other mortals—uh, players. Of course, running around in a toga and sandals would be tricky. . . .

Louise could have used those Olympian skills right then. Neither team made any big mistakes in the first half, and the ball zigged and zagged back and forth.

At the start of the fourth quarter, Louise stood on the sidelines. This was only her second substitution. Normally by this point she was running out of steam. But after two weeks of car washing, vacuuming, and basement cleaning, she was not even breathing hard.

As the ball went out of bounds, the coach called for substitutions.

"All right," she said, "we're down by one, but there's still plenty of time. Louise, go back in at right midfield. And take the throw-in."

"What about forward, Coach? I'm not tired at all."

"That's why I need you to clog up the middle."

Clog up the middle? She hadn't been doing all those chores—um, training—just to be a clog. What was the matter with the coach?

Couldn't she tell that Louise had become a sleek and powerful soccer weapon? All she needed was a chance.

"But—"

"Louise, who's the coach here? Now take the throw-in!"

Louise was so flustered that she lifted her back foot on the throw-in—and the other team got the ball. But she quickly made up for her mistake, forcing a turnover.

"Over here, Louise!"

Louise heard Megan—and chipped the ball to her on the wing. Then she sprinted downfield, receiving Megan's kick back on the give-and-go. As the defense converged on Louise, Trelawney was left alone near the goal. She waved frantically to Louise, trying to get her attention without alerting the other team.

But Louise kept her head down. Think goal, she told herself, and nothing else.

Darting past the sweeper, she dodged one fullback and spun past the other. As the goalie

charged at her, Louise chipped the ball up just beyond her reach.

GOAL!

Louise pumped her hands in the air as the crowd cheered.

On the way home, Mr. Page stole a glance at Louise in the rear-view mirror. She was staring out the window.

"You're awfully quiet, Louise," her father commented. "Wait till you tell Lionel you scored the tying goal. He'll be impressed."

"I suppose."

"I would have thought you'd be more excited than that."

Louise sighed. "Well, I wanted to be. But it's hard to be excited when your team isn't excited with you."

"The crowd cheered," her father reminded her.

"Yeah, but the crowd doesn't know that much. They're just happy to see a goal."

"And what did your team see differently?" asked Mr. Page.

Louise hesitated. She knew the answer— she just wasn't sure she wanted to say it out loud.

"Louise?"

"Well," she said slowly, "I didn't look for any help. I was kind of a ball hog." Louise sighed.

"Ah," said Mr. Page. He didn't say anything more. He didn't have to.

Louise knew what he was thinking.

CHAPTER 10

Louise hesitated as she and her mother entered the mall.

"Mother, once we're inside, do we have to walk together?"

Mrs. Page drummed her fingers on her arm. "How far apart did you have in mind? Three feet? Six? What if I just walk ten steps behind you?"

Louise considered it. "I suppose that would be all right. Thanks."

"If you're embarrassed to be seen with me," said her mother, "imagine how I feel."

"What do you mean?"

"My daughter is walking through the mall

carrying a backpack full of books. Does she
need the books at the mall? No. Are they
heavy? Yes."

"It's all part of my training," Louise
explained.

"Don't get me wrong," said her mother. "I
love our spotless garage and weeded back-
yard. I just think you're overdoing it a little."

"Not at all," said Louise, adjusting one of
the straps weighing down her shoulder. "I
feel fine."

"Just remember, we could have gone to the library. They have lots of classic books on gods and goddesses."

"No, no, this has to be a new book, something that contains new information, new insights, new . . ."

"You mean something no one else in the class already knows."

Louise smiled. "I suppose you could put it like that. I prefer to think of it as part of my never-ending search for knowledge."

Her mother smiled back.

They parted inside the bookstore, promising to meet again in a few minutes. Louise was headed for the section labeled Myths & Legends when she heard one of the clerks talking to a customer.

"It *is* a tough level. You get out on the cliff and there doesn't seem to be anywhere to go."

Even from that brief description, Louise knew exactly what he was talking about.

"I haven't seen any guides for Trek published yet."

The girl he was talking to had her back turned, but Louise could see her nodding.

"Excuse me," said Louise. "But I know Trek and I've gotten past that point. You just have to . . ."

The clerk and the customer had turned toward her. The clerk looked a little bored, but the customer . . .

"Oh. It's you, Trelawney."

She nodded. "Hi, Louise."

"Ah," said the clerk, "you two know each other? Great. See if you can put your heads together."

He moved on to help someone else.

Louise knew that while this wasn't the *most* awkward moment in her life, it was certainly awkward enough.

Aware that her cheeks were beginning to flush, Louise was surprised to see that Trelawney also looked embarrassed.

"I had no idea," said Louise.

Trelawney looked around. "About what?"

"About you and Trek. I mean, I never pictured you playing computer games."

"Oh, yes," said Trelawney. "Back home I spent hours fairly glued to the screen."

"Really? What level are you on?"

Trelawney shrugged. "Only Level 4. I keep falling off the cliff."

Louise nodded. "I was stuck there for a while too. Then I realized you have to step back and take a running leap across the Conjurer's Chasm."

"I've tried jumping off," said Trelawney. "I always end up crushed on the rocks below."

"That's because they make you think it's a dead end," Louise explained. "But actually, if you start back and leap across, the screen scrolls forward to another cliff just out of view."

"Did you figure that out yourself?"

"I guess so." Louise grinned. "Of course, I ended up on the rocks myself a few times."

Trelawney blinked. "You're terribly clever, Louise."

Louise felt her face reddening again, but this time she didn't mind at all.

CHAPTER 11

"I don't get it."

Lionel was standing outside Louise's room. Louise was lying on her bed, reading *Soccer Monthly*.

"I said, 'I DON'T GET IT'!"

Louise lowered her magazine. "You don't get what, Lionel? You have to be more specific. After all, there are many things you don't get."

"I'm talking about Trelawney."

"What about her?"

"All of a sudden you're spending lots of time with her."

"So?"

"So I thought you didn't like her."

Louise smiled at him. "That just shows how little you know me, Lionel."

Lionel folded his arms. "Come on, Louise, tell the truth. What's your master plan? I'll bet it's something really sneaky."

"Sorry, Lionel. Go fish. I'm not planning—"

"Louise!" Mrs. Page called out from downstairs. "Trelawney's here!"

"Here!" Lionel gasped.

Louise ignored him and got up to greet her guest.

"Flee!" cried Lionel. "Run for your lives!"

"That's my little brother," Louise explained. "Say good-bye, Lionel."

"Good-bye, Lionel. I should tell you, though," he added to Trelawney. "I don't usually talk to myself like this."

Trelawney nodded. "That's good."

"Welcome to my world," said Louise. "How about a snack? I think we have some triple fudge ice cream."

"Scrumptious," said Trelawney. "We never had more than single fudge at home." She blinked suddenly.

Louise knew that look. It was the same one she had seen in the mirror after her first week at sleepaway camp.

"I guess it's hard settling in a new place," Louise said softly.

After polishing off their ice cream, the two girls sat down to play Trek on the computer.

Louise watched as Trelawney entered the Forbidden Swamp.

"That's perfect," said Louise. "Now pay attention around this next corner. One of the crocodiles is waiting there. Look closely, you can see his shadow."

Trelawney nodded, her eyes scanning across the screen.

"Now dart to the right and stop short. See the crocodile following you? He can't turn as fast as you can. So he keeps going—straight into the quicksand."

"Hurrah!" cried Trelawney, beaming. "I can't tell you how many times that croc did me in."

"It's all about timing," Louise explained. "You have to wait for the, um, *croc* to react before you make your move."

Trelawney nodded. "I never quite thought of it that way. It's really rather like how I think during a football match." She grinned. "I mean, a soccer game. You know, Louise, if you took the same sense of timing you showed here and put it on the soccer field, you could be amazing."

Louise blushed. "Really?"

"Oh, yes. You already have the moves. And you're obviously well trained. All you have to do is think beyond yourself. Just imagine the field as a giant computer screen with pieces moving around."

"Hmmm . . ."

"You just have to anticipate different moves. With a little practice, I think you could definitely surprise people."

Louise nodded. "I'd like that. People are always accusing me of being too predictable."

"Me too. 'We can always see you coming, Trelawney,' they say. 'You're as clear as glass.'"

Louise nodded. "Who do they think they are?"

"Quite right."

"Well, maybe if we work together, and practiced some plays, we could *both* surprise the team."

Trelawney smiled. "*I'd* like that," she said.

CHAPTER 12

It was late in the second half, and Louise couldn't help feeling that she had played this game before. The moves, the action—it all seemed so familiar.

Of course! This was almost exactly like her dream, the one where she was all alone and ready to score. But this was no dream. Her parents really were on the sidelines cheering, and her teammates were rushing into position.

"Shoot, Louise!" Megan screamed at her.

Louise had a shot, she could see that.

"Louise, come on! Time's running out!"

This came from Emily.

Louise waited. She knew she had a shot, but it wasn't a great one. But if she could just wait for the defense to collapse on her . . .

Imagine the field as a giant computer screen.

"Louise, watch out!"

But Louise *was* watching. As the sweeper bore down on her, cutting her angle to the goal, her chance to shoot vanished. But shooting wasn't what Louise had in mind.

"You snooze, you lose," said the sweeper, creeping closer.

Louise opened her arms to shrug—and chipped the ball gently toward the middle.

The startled sweeper leapt up, but the ball sailed just out of reach . . . and fell to where Trelawney was waiting.

The two girls had practiced this play for hours and hours. Trelawney had helped Louise understand that it was just like in Trek where you had to lure the gremlins into the pit so you could jump over them to safety. And Louise had helped her make that jump.

As the ball hit the ground, Trelawney trapped it neatly. Then she whirled around—and fired.

GOAL!

The whole team erupted in a giant cheer, and Louise joined in loudly. Hera and Athena, she thought, couldn't have done any better.

Tweeeet!

The referee blew her whistle—and the game was over.

The Pages rushed over from the sidelines to congratulate the winning team.

"Louise looked great out there," Megan's father said to Mr. Page.

"Thanks. I've been giving her pointers."

Mrs. Page laughed.

Louise was glad to see them, even Lionel. But his expression puzzled her.

"What's the matter, Lionel? You look disappointed."

"Gee, Louise," said Lionel, "I'm glad you

won and everything. But I thought you were going to do a rainbow or something."

"Well, Lionel," Louise said with a smile, "I guess that's just the way the ball bounces—and bounces back!"

And with that, she sprinted off to join the victory celebration.